ANAIAH LEARNS TO INVEST

Building Collette-Anaiah's susu box

Author: Anaiah Akosua Ofori-Poku
Illustrator: Nana Ama Buabeng-Munkoh

Assistant Authors: Vivian Kwakyewaa Ofori
and Gerda Owusu Agyapong

tellwell

Tellwell Talent
www.tellwell.ca

ISBN
978-0-2288-5733-4 (Paperback)

Dedication

I dedicate this book to my mom, Vivian Ofori, and to my extended family (you know who you are). Daddy, I love you very much, thanks for everything. I also give a special shoutout to all the kids who are unafraid to believe in themselves.

One beautiful day, I saw my mother's busy fingers twirling around and moving things in the house as she talked on the phone. I was surprised to overhear her talk about wanting to buy a new house to live in. She said she wanted to rent out our current home (that I love so much) as an investment.

"Investment? What is that?" I cried out loud, feeling sad and curious. I shook my head and refused to move. I could not understand my mother's plans as she tried to explain them to me. So, I decided to make it my job to find out what an investment is.

I asked almost everyone who phoned my mom what "investment" means. The grown ups tried their very best however, some of the big words that were used confuse me even more. I still didn't know what an "investment" was, and I still didn't want to move.

This went on for days until I saw Mom talking to one of my favourite uncles, Uncle Collins.

Uncle Collins never calls me by my given name, Anaiah. To Uncle Collins, I was named after him, so he always calls me Collette. If anyone knew what investment means, I thought it would be Uncle Collins. So, I asked,

"Uncle Collins, what is an investment?"

"Collette, I have a challenge for you. If you come up with a business idea I like, I will "invest" in it to show you exactly what investment means."
After accepting the challenge to come up with a business idea for Uncle Collins to invest in, I wandered around the entire house. I tried to be creative but no ideas came to me.

First, I thought of becoming a cooking host, but I wondered about all the cleaning of dishes I would have to do. Then I thought it would be cool to have a talk show on YouTube, but then I realized I have no camera. Finally, my mom and Aunt Flings advised me to create a business in something that I love and know so well.

Kids cooking show

COOKING WITH KIDS

Learn about Ghana

ings & I

Mum & I

Whats our talent?

what do you love doing?

Tools and materials

Anaiah's business ideas brainstorming session

Hours involved

Time

inspiration

GIRLPODCAST
AWESOME SLOGAN

Savings

Painting class

Supervision

Podcast

My mom reminded me that I have known how to save money since I was five years old. Aunt Flings also reminded me how much I love painting.
At that moment, I knew I could combine the two things I loved to create Collette-Anaiah susu boxes.

Susu means savings in the Ghanaian Akan dialect. Influenced by my Ghanaian heritage, I came up with the idea of customized saving piggy boxes to teach other kids how to be disciplined savers.

That way, we can all be smart savers
now and when we grow up.

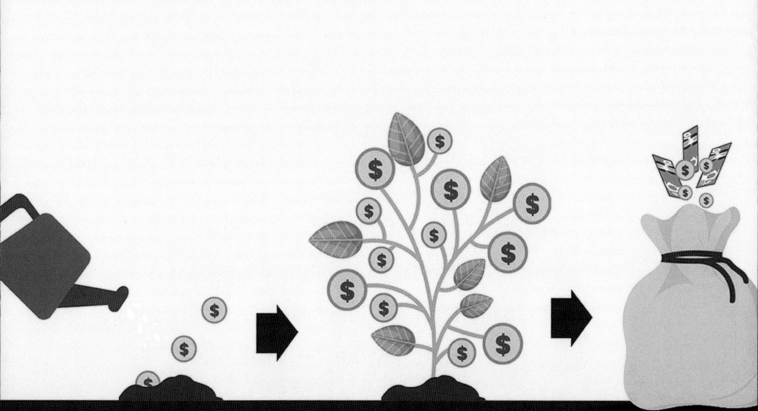

I showed my mom and my entire family how much I wanted to create something cool so that Uncle Collins would invest in my business.

Everyone in my family loved the idea. They encouraged me and cheered me on. My sugar mama helped me create a vision board to bring my business to life. Auntie Flings helped me choose bright colours and traditional styles from Ghana to design my susu boxes.

On the presentation day, everyone who knew about my business idea called to see if I was ready to show off my hard work. I was so nervous that I could not keep it together.

Aunt Ann, who was so invested in my business from the start, called to see how I was doing. It's like she already knew how nervous I was. She helped calm my nerves and encouraged me by saying, "You got this."

Auntie Ann is a social worker for school-aged kids. She spent some time doing calming activities with me to remind me of my goals and how strong my mind is. She used all her skills to invest in my emotional well-being.

I gathered enough courage and finally presented my business to Uncle Collins, Aunt Flings, and Mom. They were so proud that they decided to invest their time and resources in my new business.

In the end, I learned so much more about investment. I learned that investment can be a financial gain. An investment can come from extended and immediate family members supporting you financially and emotionally with their time and resources. My mother ended up buying the house to use as a financial investment for my future. But that's a story for another day!

THE END

Through the lens of a child, readers see Anaiah taking on a new challenge of learning the meaning of investment while motivating other kids to do the same. Learning how to invest at an early age is important for kids to experience how the world works early on.

Manufactured by Amazon.ca
Bolton, ON